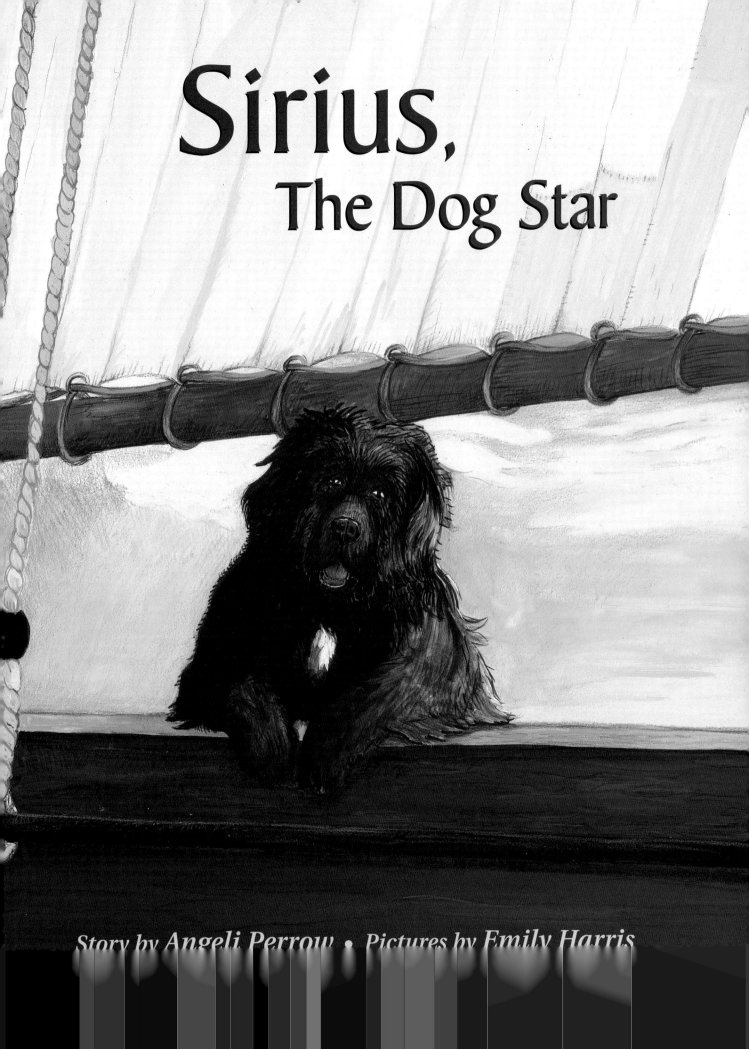

Sirius,
The Dog Star

Story by Angeli Perrow • Pictures by Emily Harris

Story © 2002 by Angeli Perrow

Illustrations © 2002 by Emily Harris

Library of Congress Control Number: 2002106576

ISBN 0-89272-545-1

Printed in China / OGP

2   4   5   3   1

Down East Books / Camden, Maine

www.downeastbooks.com

For Mark, with whom life is an adventure. — A.P.

For my parents and John, with love. — E.H.

"Star light, star bright, first star I see tonight . . ." chanted Nathan to the big Newfoundland dog beside him.

It was a cold, clear night off the coast of Maine. Boy and dog gazed at the darkening sky as the stars blinked on, one by one. Nathan gripped the rail of the *Goldhunter* and tipped his head back.

"Look! There's Orion, the Hunter. Follow the three stars in his belt southeast to Canis Major—that's Latin for 'the Big Dog.' And that star there, the brightest one of all, is Sirius."

When he heard his name, Sirius barked and waved his tail like a feathery flag. He raised a webbed paw, as big as a bear's foot, to shake.

Nathan laughed. "That's right, Sirius. You are the Dog Star."

At sunrise the sea was calm—a mirror of the fiery sky. "Red at night, sailors' delight. Red in the morning, sailors take warning," Nathan recited. "Means weather's a-brewin'."

As the day grew older, the waves grew higher. The schooner began to buck like an untamed horse.

"Batten the hatches!" commanded the captain.

Nathan and the crew lashed and tied, dashed and tried to secure the cargo.

A huge wave, bigger than any that had come before, lifted the bow of the ship. The sailors hung on with all their might. Water, cold as a winter river, rushed across the deck, sweeping every loose thing into the sea.

Sirius floundered in the flood, floating ever nearer the edge. Nathan watched, eyes wide with horror. That big Newfie was his best friend. He had to save him.

The boy looped a line around the mast. He seized it and skittered across the slanting deck. He grabbed the dog's collar, threaded the line through, and tied it with a square knot. Now Sirius was safe. The dog licked Nathan's face to say thanks.

The wind was rising. It moaned in the ship's rigging like an injured animal. The *Goldhunter* wallowed in the wild waves as breaker after breaker battered her bow.

Nathan grasped the mast with desperate hands. Fear stabbed at his heart. He had never seen waves bigger or wind fiercer.

And he was cold—so cold. Ice was forming on his face and clothes. Small ice balls clung to the dog's whiskers and fur. Ice was forming on the ship, weighing it down.

Suddenly, there was a *thud,* and the schooner began to tip.

"We've struck a ledge!" cried the captain. "Abandon ship!"

Nathan's numb fingers fumbled with the line that held
Sirius to the mast. He retied the end around his own belt.
Now they were bound together, friends to the end.

They leaped into the lifeboat. A rising billow lifted the
dory away from the sinking ship.

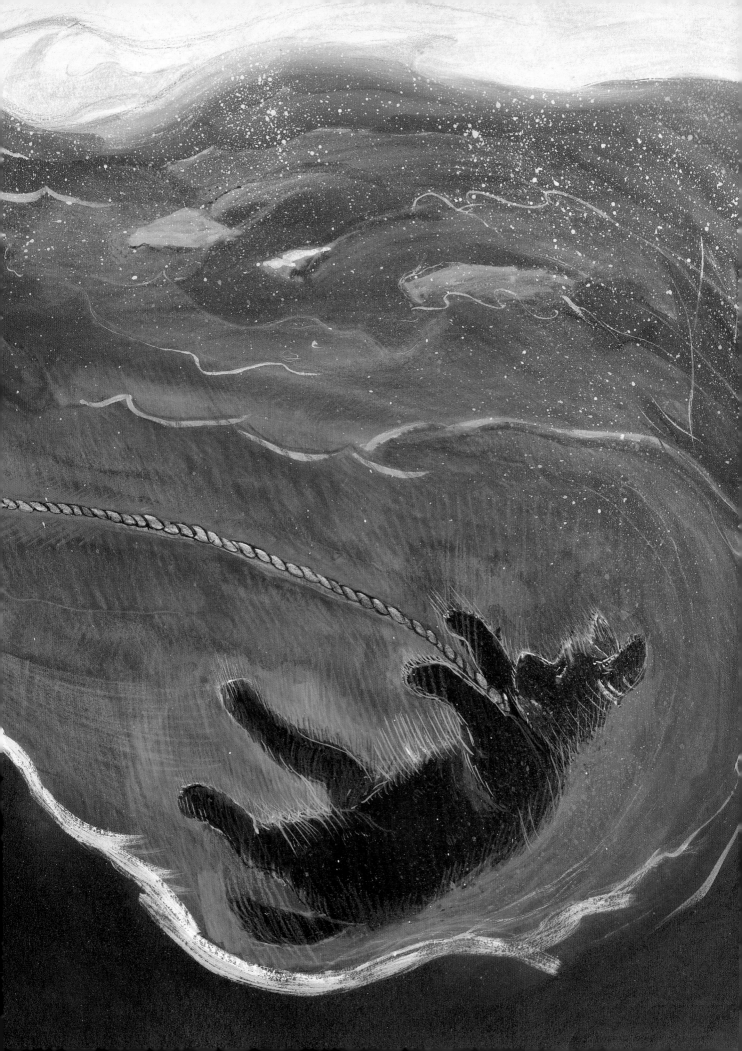

The little boat tossed this way and that in the raging sea. Night was coming. Boy and dog huddled in the bow.

"Oh, Sirius, what shall we do?" Nathan whispered.

Suddenly Sirius barked. Nathan glanced up and saw a glint in the distance. "A light, sir. A light!" he called to the captain.

All eyes strained to see.

"It's Boon Island Light," the captain exclaimed. "We'll be safe, if only we can reach it!"

The men rowed wearily toward the light. For six long, dark hours they battled the wind and waves.

At last the tower of Boon Island Lighthouse loomed above them. The surf boomed on the jagged rocks.

"How shall we land, sir?" asked one of the crewmen. "The dory will be smashed to pieces if we try to get closer."

While the captain considered this problem, Sirius began to bark. He barked and he barked.

Soon lanterns appeared on the shore—it
was the lighthouse keeper and his son!
"Follow our lanterns!" shouted Keeper
Williams. He and his son, Charles, trudged to
the other side of the island, where the surf
was calmer.

The exhausted sailors used their last bit of strength to row around the island.

Still there were rocks, as hungry as shark's teeth.

"Come in on the fourth sea!" Keeper Williams directed.

Nathan knew that meant every fourth wave was higher than the rest. His heart was thumping. The men were weak and nearly frozen. They no longer had the strength to swing the boat in time to catch the highest wave. They needed a miracle.

Then Nathan had an idea. Sirius was strong and brave— and a good swimmer. Could Nathan send his friend into the sea? It was their only chance.

"Jump, Sirius. Jump!" Nathan commanded.
The big dog leaped into the water. A wave broke over him,
and he disappeared.

Nathan held his breath. Then the dog's head bobbed to the surface. The boy tossed the bow line to Sirius. The dog caught it in his teeth and paddled in place, waiting.

Nathan counted the waves. "One . . . two . . . three . . . and here comes . . . FOUR! Go, Sirius! GO!"

With strong strokes, the Newfie splashed toward shore, his tail straight behind him like a rudder. The wave lifted the dory over the last of the dangerous rocks and onto solid ground.

Sirius scrambled across the slabs of sea ice
and presented the bow line to Keeper Williams.

Strong hands pulled the dory to safety. The keepers lifted the frozen men out of the boat and carried them to the lighthouse, one by one.

Later, after everyone had thawed out, the men talked about the rescue. "We heard the dog barking," explained Keeper Williams. "Otherwise, we would not have known you were out there. He is one amazing dog."

"He sure is!" exclaimed Nathan proudly. "He's Sirius, the Dog Star.'"

AUTHOR'S NOTE

*T*he shipwreck of the Goldhunter *took place at Boon Island Ledge on December 3, 1897, about three miles from the lighthouse. Boon Island Light, off the southern Maine coast, is one of America's most remote and dangerous lighthouse stations.*

Years later, the former lightkeeper, William Williams, wrote in a letter to author Edward Rowe Snow that the temperature was "four below zero, and it was a thick vapor, and blowing a gale of wind from the northwest....We were awakened by the barking of a dog, of all things....Getting out our lanterns,...we shouted to the men to follow the light around the rocks to the lee of the island....When the boat came closer, we watched as the dog leaped into the water with the painter in his teeth [and] scrambled and skidded ashore over the ice to present that bow line to us."* A fourteen-year-old black crewman was among the sailors Keeper Williams rescued that day.

The name and breed of the heroic dog are not known. However, it is very possible that he was a Newfoundland. These majestic dogs were often found on sailing ships. Newfies are famous for their strength, swimming ability, and willingness to rescue anyone in trouble.

*Edward Rowe Snow, Fantastic Folklore and Fact *(Dodd, Mead & Co., 1968).*